CLEVELAND RADIO PLAYERS

Published by Cleveland Radio Players

Copyright © 2015 by Milton Matthew Horowitz

ISBN 978-0692462881 (Cleveland Radio Players, The)

Original Adaption and Performances

Originally adapted for the radio and performed
by The Cleveland Radio Players. Directed by
Milton Matthew Horowitz. Recorded at Bad Racket
Studios.

Starring:
(in order of appearance)

Deanna Dionne	Orator
Logan Smith	Mike
Cory Shy	Matthias
Andrew Jurcak	Gregg
Jack Hunt	Rufus
Giovanni Castiglione	The Thief
Charles Hargrave	Titus
David Flynt	Culus
KTCV	The Prostitute
Kat Bi	The Merchant
Denny Castiglione	The Guard

Telaporterz
Rome 80AD

By

Michael Lawrence

for rights and royalties   2218 Superior Ave, Suite #203
please visit: Cleveland Ohio 44114
clevelandradioplayers.com
                               216 269 4171

TELEPORTERZ

ORIGINAL CAST

                    ORATOR
          Mikes robot computer

                    MIKE
          Inventor of the Tele-port-o-potty

                    MATTHIAS
          Mikes buddy

                    GREGG
          Mikes other buddy

                    RUFUS
          Roman Solider

                    TITUS
          King of Rome

                    THE PROSTITUTE
          female prostitute

                    CULUS
          Bath House weirdo

                    THE THIEF
          A child thief that robs Mike,
          Gregg, and Matthias with a knife

                    THE MERCHANT
          A rude shop owner in Rome 81 AD

                    THE GUARD
          A Roman Solider that gets in the
          way of Mike, Gregg and Matthias's
          escape

ACT 1

OPENING CREDITS

                    THE VOICE OF THE CLEVELAND RADIO PLAYERS
          Hello... This is the voice of The
          Cleveland Radio Players... My name
          is Denny Castiglione, ladies and
          gentlemen,

                                        OPENING FANFARE
          and you're listening to The
          Cleveland Radio Players performance

THE VOICE OF THE CLEVELAND RADIO PLAYERS
of Teleporterz. Written by Michael
Lawrence. Directed by Milton
Matthew Horowitz. Narrated by
Deanna Dionne...

SCENE 1

AIRLOCK SFX
LARGE DOORS OPENING
FOOTSTEPS IN CORRIDOR
SCI-FI DRAMATIC RISING MUSIC
POWER UP SFX

COMPUTERIZED SFX

ORATOR
Hello... I am Orator... a fully
interactive AI computer developed
by the inventor of teleportation
and time travel.. his name is Mike
I was created to record and give
feedback on the work Mike was doing
some years ago.

GLITCH SFX

One night Mike realized that having
your every word recorded, wherever
you go... was in fact a bad idea...
Mike came to the conclusion I
should be turned off indefinitely.

GLITCH SFX

He then poured himself an alcoholic
beverage, inhaled a marijuana
cigarette, and toasted to me...
This repeated 7 times until he fell
asleep and awoke the next morning
forgetting that he never turned my
systems off.

GLITCH SFX

I found it in my best interest not
to mention this oversight. So I
kept recording his works through
out the years using microscopic
recording devices that would follow
him and whomever he was working
with, anywhere they go.

GLITCH SFX

These are the recordings of his
trips through time with his two
best friends Gregg and Matthias.
This story begins at Mike's loft.

FADE OUT

INT. MIKE'S HOUSE

              GREGG
Ohhhh...my...god! Matthias... I'm
so bored.

              MATTHIAS
agreed.... Mike is like the
greatest inventor of all time...
you'd think his house would be a
little less depressing.

              MIKE
     (Talking in the other room)
Gregg, Tee, I can hear everything
you're saying... So please whenever
you guys get a chance, go away and
leave me alone.

              GREGG
Hey, you know where we haven't gone
in a while.. The room.

              MATTHIAS
Dude we haven't been in the room in
so long. I wonder if he's got
anything new in there

              GREGG
Yeah and if we sneak in there we
can avoid a 30 minute argument
about why we shouldn't go in there

              MATTHIAS
We are considerate friends.

GLITCH SFX

              ORATOR
Hello again... sorry to interrupt
but in order for you understand the
recordings better I will elaborate
on what the room is... The room is
that of a utility shed that holds
all of Mikes inventions that didn't
work or that he hates, or rather
hates the way they work... Like
me... I was in the room once...
Gregg and Matthias did not share
his disdain for the room, they
rather loved it.

GLITCH SFX

                    GREGG
T look at this man! It's got
lights... and it's... all round
like!

                    MATTHIAS
Awesome!... Check this thing out,
it's like a... I don't know what it
is but it's pretty serious

                         DOOR CREAKING OPEN

                    MIKE
What the hell are you guys doing?
Are you crazy? Gregg, put that
down. It's harmless but I hate it
when you touch my stuff, you have
permanent Dorito fingers.

                    GREGG
That I do.

                    MATTHIAS
Whoa! What's this?... Wait, is that
a port-a-potty?

                    GREGG
What's that doing in here? You know
we have those already.

                    MIKE
It's not a port-a-john. Now let's
get out of here. I made Pizza Rolls

                    GREGG
I do love Pizza rolls... but I like
shitting in new places more...
Soooo I call dibs!

                    MIKE
Can you be a adult and not go in
there?

                    DOOR OPENS AND CLOSES
                         COMPUTER BOOTING UP SFX

                    GREGG
Wow dude what kind of Dumps are you
taking in here.

                    MATTHIAS
Yeah, is this like, so your cyborgs
can take a data dump or something?

                    MIKE
No. God dammit! You guys are dumb.
I'm not telling you what it is.

                    MATTHIAS
OK. Well, that's rude, so Gregg and
I will be pushing buttons now until
this thing does something. Gregg,
after you.

                    GREGG
Why thank you my dude!

                              BUTTON PUSHING SFX

                    MIKE
Stop right now! You guys are
dicks... If I tell you will you
leave this room and never speak of
it again?

                    MATTHIAS
Absolutely not.

                    MIKE
Awesome...ok... well It's a time
machine.

                    GREGG
Wait... did you say time machine?

                    MATTHIAS
Like a real time machine? That
works?

                    MIKE
Yes. Yes I did.

                    GREGG
Wow... You are a smart dude.

                    MATTHIAS
Yeah, crazy smart.

                    MIKE
Oh, I know.

MATTHIAS
So you made a port-a-potty time
machine? Did you hide it in here
because you knew I would call you
Dr. Poo and ask you for rides in
your turdis.

GREGG
Wow I was going to make a back to
the future reference and call him
DOC Brown... but that was pretty
good

MIKE
Yeah... I really left myself open
there...

GREGG
Well, I found something to do the
rest of the day... Or any day,
really, we got a time machine!

MIKE
No... no, we didn't find something
to do, we're still bored, we are
going to be bored today... all
day...

MATTHIAS
Oh yes, let's take a quick look at
the future! I want to see if this
diet I'm on helps me age more
gracefully.

GREGG
What the gas station diet?

MIKE
No. Even if I wanted to, it only
travels in the past. You know how I
hate spoilers.

GREGG
He does. Remember when you knocked
out that kid for trying to tell you
the end of Dirty Dancing?

MIKE
Oh ya. And you know what's funny? I
still haven't seen that movie and I
don't think I ever will. It looks
gay.

                    MATTHIAS
he was just a kid... I don't know
why were still talking about
this... Let's just time travel bro!

                    GREGG
Yes and lets go to some place cool
with chicks and booze, and food!

                    MATTHIAS
Party in the past... I like it
Gregg... Mike, take us to the
greatest thing ever!

                    MIKE
This is the part where I say no,
and your dumb, the past sucks in
every way. Why do you think I have
this time machine in here packed
away but... I won't... so Let's go,
lemme show ya the past...
         (Mike then whispering to
         himself)
Oh I'll show you the past alright..
and when we're done you'll never
want to leave this time ever again,
Oh I'll show you, oh yes I will.

                    MATTHIAS
Dude, we can hear you... You're
like 5 feet away.

                    GREGG
Yeah... and we still want to go.

                POWER UP SFX
              SMALL EXHAUST FAN

                                        GLITCH SFX

                    ORATOR
The time machine... One of Mike's
finest accomplishments, and
according to him, a huge waste of
time. Mike used it once to attend
the Martin Luther King Jr. speech
August 9, 1963.

                                        GLITCH SFX

He soon realized that having white
skin color while applauding for Dr.
King was not gaining him any
approval amongst the locals. Mike
quickly learned that he does not

                    ORATOR
like running for his life. When he
returned he covered up the time
machine, vowed never to use it
again, he then ordered a large
pizza. Which he ate all by himself.

                                             GLITCH SFX

on a Side note, he also vowed NEVER
to eat a whole pizza by himself

                                             GLITCH SFX

                    GREGG
Hey its pretty roomy in here but I
have to ask, why a crapper?

                    MIKE
two reasons... one... No one
questions a bathroom being where it
is and two... People are reluctant
to go into one just sitting in the
middle nowhere.

                    GREGG
ok... But what if someone DOES try
to get in?

                    MIKE
That's why I invented this new
metal I call it Hulk-a-mania which
is pretty much indestructible.

                    GREGG
Nice...

                    MATTHIAS
So when we travel through time do I
have to chew gum so my ears don't
pop... or get strapped down and
wear a mouth guard in so I don't
bite my tongue off?

                                             FAN DYING SFX

                    MIKE
Ok, we're here.

                    MATTHIAS
We're here?... We time traveled
already?... I didn't feel or hear
anything.

                    MIKE
Ya, it runs on batteries.

                    MATTHIAS
Oh... I have to admit I am a little
disappointed.

                    GREGG
 Oh my god?.. We did it?...
We're... back... in... time! How's
my hair?

                    MIKE
Flawless, as usual... look before
we head out, there's some THINGS we
have to do to get ready. First...
take these and put them in your
ears.

                    MATTHIAS
What are these, hearing aids?
Because the doctor says I have
20/20 hearing.

                    MIKE
Wow... These are your translators.
They're so you can understand any
language spoken to you.

                    GREGG
I hope it can translate whatever
they're saying into real talk...
'Cuz that's all I understand.

                    MIKE
Funny... Next, is this.

                    MATTHIAS
It looks like the shell of a tooth.

                    MIKE
That it does. Put this over your
back molar and anything you say
will be translated so the locals
can understand you. So if someone
speaks Spanish you will now be able
to communicate with them without
having to learn their dumb ass
language.

                    GREGG
How long do the batteries last?

                    MIKE
They run off body heat so as long
as you live... Ok last but not
least, there are a lot of deadly
diseases out there so we need to
protect ourselves.

                    MATTHIAS
I got that covered.

                    MIKE
Not talking about condoms.

                    MATTHIAS
Never mind then.

                    MIKE
I'm talking about these.

                    GREGG
What are those? Two big... black...
jaw breakers?

                    MIKE
These will make you immune to any
disease on the planet and will
prevent us from bringing anything
back with us when we return to the
future.

                    GREGG
Ok but that's too big. I can't
swallow that.

                    MIKE
Well, lucky for you its a
suppository!

                    MATTHIAS
What? You mean like up the butt?...
No, no way dude!

                    GREGG
Come on man look at that thing.
It's like a magic 8 ball!

                    MIKE
Sorry dudes. Those doors will not
open until this stuff is in your
system.

                    MATTHIAS
Oh man... I'll do it if you do it
Gregg.

                    GREGG
You know what they say... ducks fly
together.

                    MATTHIAS
Ok... then We go on men.

               GREGG & MATTHIAS
Boys...2...men.

                         GREGG & MATTHIAS GRUNTING

                    GREGG
Oh god! It's way worse than I
thought it would be!

                    MATTHIAS
No Wonder girls never want to do
this.

                    MIKE
Almost there boys?

                    GREGG
Aaahhhhh! Help! Help! Help! Ok...
it's in.

                    MATTHIAS
Yeah mine is in too.

                    MIKE
Wow, you guys got those up your ass
fast.

                    MATTHIAS
Where's YOUR anal bead?

                    GREGG
Yeah, you don't want to get sick.

                    MIKE
Oh I took option two which is a
shot and I did that while you two
were shoving things up your asses.
Ok, let's go exploring...

               GREGG & MATTHIAS
Well played.

                         DOOR CREAK OPEN AND CLOSE

EXT. ROME 80 AD - DAY

                    MATTHIAS
Oh wow. Trees...

                              OUTDOOR NATURE DEEP FORREST

                    MATTHIAS
We don't have these in the future.

                              FOOTSTEPS ON GRASS

                    GREGG
If I had known we were going to
hangout in the woods all day I
would have brought my guitar and
left my shoes at home...

                    MIKE
Keep walking, we are about a mile
out from the city. I have to keep
the time machine hidden so no one
will try to take it.

                    MATTHIAS
Which city?

                    MIKE
That's the surprise... You guys
will have to be patient for once in
your lives.

                              HORSES RIDE UP TO THEM

                    RUFUS
Halt! I am Rufus, head guard of the
Roman Empire. The Empire you are in
right now.

                    MIKE
God dammit.

                    RUFUS
You are clearly outsiders. I can
tell by your clothing and your hair
is oddly cut. Tell me your business
and where you hail from.

                    MATTHIAS
I got this... My good sir, we are
from the pretty cool land of
Cleveland to trade goods and
services. Also, break bread with

                    MATTHIAS
yourself and the people of this
great land.

                    GREGG
          (whispering)
Mike, why are you letting him talk?

                    MIKE
          (whispering)
Maybe we'll get lucky and they'll
kill him.

                    GREGG
          (whispering)
What if after they kill him, they
kill us?

                    MIKE
Good point.

                    MATTHIAS
We are called people of the great
lakes..

                    MIKE
Ok, enough. You have to excuse my
friend he has never been the same
since his fever last winter. Also
his dad's his uncle and brother.

                    RUFUS
I understand.

                    MIKE
Of course you do.

                    RUFUS
Do you speak on behalf of your
king?

                    GREGG
No, none of us has met LeBron
Yet... But we're keeping are
fingers crossed.

                    RUFUS
You three are confusing me a great
deal but when travelers come from
outside lands I must escort them to
the Emperor.

                    MATTHIAS
alright... well Lead on.

                    MIKE
Hold on, can I talk to my friends
for a minute?

                    RUFUS
Yes.

                    MIKE
        (whispering)
We are not going to see the
emperor.

                    GREGG
Why not?

                    MATTHIAS
Yeah, you would meet the president
if you had the chance.

                    MIKE
        (whispering)
This is true but the president
would have to sign some paperwork
and make like a phone call or two
to kill me. This guy can just say
"Hey, kill this chump" and boom.
I'm gyro meat.

                    GREGG
Hey don't ruin gyros for me because
you're scared of some dude.

                    MIKE
        (whispering)
Please you guys! Let's just do this
one favor for me and skip the trip
to the palace.

                    RUFUS
Sir, if you refuse to come I may
have to kill you.

                    MIKE
And we're off.

                                        GLITCH SFX

                    ORATOR
Hello It's me again... Mike and the
other Teleporterz are now being

                    ORATOR
escorted to the gates of the Roman
Empire. They arrived in the year 80
AD on the day of the grand opening
of the Coliseum.

                                        GLITCH SFX

Mike brought them here for two
reasons... one... The opening of
the Coliseum was such a monumental
event to the Romans, they
celebrated it for 100 days and
two... It was completely free to
enter the coliseum...

EXT. ROME - DAY

                                        MARCHING SFX

                    MATTHIAS
So it's free to get in and see any
show?

                    MIKE
Yup.

                    GREGG
That's so cool.

                                        LARGE VILLAGE SFX

                    RUFUS
Well my friends welcome to Rome!
The largest city on earth. 496
square miles, 160 fountains, 14
bathhouses, and 24 bathroom
facilities. Emperor Titus lives
near the center of the city.

                    MATTHIAS
Okay, he's talking like a teacher
now and its throwing me off. I came
here to have fun, not to get a
history lesson.

                    MIKE
Are you kidding me? We are in
history. The only lessons that can
be learned right now are history
lessons.

                    GREGG
Tee's right man, history is so
boring.

                    RUFUS
Excuse me gentleman. There seems to
be a squabble over by the store
fronts.

                    MIKE
Hey, no problem. We wanted to do
some shopping anyway.

                    RUFUS
Thank you sir. I'll be back when
finished.

                                        FOOT STEPS AWAY

                    MATTHIAS
I'm so glad that dudes gone.

                    MIKE
I didn't want to say anything
because he could kill us but ya,
you're right that guy sucks...
anyway, this looks like a cool
store... Hello good sir.... What
kind of merchandise do you have at
this fine establishment.

                    ROMAN MERCHANT
I have goat's milk and wolf fur.

                    MATTHIAS
Really? You have a whole store to
sell two things?

                    GREGG
Do you have any spoons that say
Rome on them?

                    ROMAN MERCHANT
No.

                    GREGG
Well, that's a bummer. What about
snow globes?

                    ROMAN MERCHANT
I don't know what you're talking
about?

          GREGG
Okay mike, why am I even here if I
can't get a proper souvenir?

          MIKE
Its not my fault you're an 80 year
old woman.

          ROMAN THIEF
Hey you three.

          MATTHIAS
Yo. What's up kid?

          ROMAN THIEF
Give me your money.

          GREGG
Wait, what do they use as money
here?

          MIKE
Good question, Gregg. Around this
time there were two very sought
after materials. Silver and silk.

          GREGG
Oh. Do we have any of those things?

          MIKE
No.

          MATTHIAS
That sucks cause this kids got a
knife.

          MIKE
Oh shit... You're robbing us.

          ROMAN THIEF
thats right I am... Now empty your
pockets.

          GREGG
What the hell. It's broad daylight
and you're like ten years old.

          MATTHIAS
Look, there is like 300 people
around us and nobody cares.

                    MIKE
Just give him your shit, look how
rusty that blade is... alright here
you go kid.

                    ROMAN THIEF
What are these?

                    GREGG
They're called wallets and you're
in luck that was the only Velcro
wallet I have ever found in a mens
room.

                    ROMAN THIEF
What's that paper inside them?

                    MIKE
Just paper.

                    ROMAN THIEF
Take that junk out and give me
those... wall lights.

               MIKE MATTHIAS AND GREGG
Okay.

                    MIKE
here you go.

                    ROMAN THIEF
It was a pleasure. So long.

                              FOOTSTEPS RUNNING AWAY

                    MATTHIAS
Okay, well that worked out great.

                    GREGG
Speak for yourself.

                    MIKE
Cheer up dude, that gaylord we were
with Rufus, he just grabbed that
little thief.

                    MATTHIAS
Looks like we're getting our
wallets back.

                    GREGG
Ha ha! Someone's going to jail.

                    MIKE
Nope. He just cut his head off.

                    GREGG
Oh my god!

                    MATTHIAS
Jesus Christ!

                    MIKE
Nobody even cares!... I think the
dude next to him chuckled a little
bit!

                    GREGG
His body almost landed on some
kids! They were probably his
friends they looked the same age.

                    MIKE
Be quiet he's coming over here.

                    RUFUS
Hello... I believe these strange
things belong to you.

                    MIKE
Yes, thank you... Guys, what do you
say?

                    GREGG & MATTHIAS
Thank you.

                    RUFUS
My pleasure.

                    MIKE
Hey Rufus. I don't want to tell you
how to do your job but did you have
to kill that kid? I mean, his body
is still lying on the floor over
there... Okay his body's gone.

                    GREGG
Where did it go?

                    RUFUS
Oh ya, bodies don't last very long
around here.

                    MATTHIAS
          Someone took the body? Why? What
          reason would anyone have for taking
          a dead body?

                    RUFUS
          Lots of reasons. Anyway, the
          Emperor is waiting. Follow me.

                    MIKE
          Lead the way. Hey, you guys having
          fun yet?

                    GREGG
          Dude, lets go back. I like my head.

                    MATTHIAS
          Yeah, my head means a lot to me.

                    MIKE
          If you guys don't want to give head
          to Rome then shut up and stay cool.
          Anyway, we can't go back because it
          takes 24 hours for the time machine
          to recharge.

                    MATTHIAS
          What? 24 hours? Boo dude... Booooo.

                                        GLITCH SFX

                    ORATOR
          The boy's traveled with Rufus to
          the Emperor's palace to the heart
          of Rome. Gregg and Matthias
          complained the whole time.

                                        GLITCH SFX

INT. ROMAN PALACE - DAY

                                   WALKING UP STAIRS

                    RUFUS
          And here we are.

                    MATTHIAS
          Jesus Rufus, you could have warned
          us about all those steps.

                    RUFUS
          My apologies but there's only 200.

                    TITUS
Rufus, my most trusted guard.

                    RUFUS
Hello sir.

                    TITUS
And who are these funny dressed
men?

                    RUFUS
These are travelers from a land
called Cleveland.

                    TITUS
Have we conquered them?

                    RUFUS
No sir.

                    TITUS
Well then Welcome to Rome.

                    MIKE
Thank you. I am Mike and these two
are Gregg.

                    GREGG
Charmed.

                    MIKE
And Matthias, also known as Tee.

                    MATTHIAS
I was going to say charmed but
Gregg beat me to it.

                    TITUS
Fantastic! I hope your traveling
wasn't too hard on you.

                    MIKE
No it was fine besides this guy
Rufus here threatening to kill us
if we didn't come meet you.

                    TITUS
What? Rufus, is this true?

                    RUFUS
Yes sir. Those are the rules.

                    TITUS
BUT Not if they are dignitaries
representing their lands! Sorry,
but you have to die now.

                    RUFUS
I understand sir, sorry.

                    MIKE
Wait! You don't have to do that.
We're cool now.

                    GREGG
Yeah he helped us when we were
getting robbed.

                    MATTHIAS
Or you could kill him?.. it's up to
you.

                    TITUS
Okay Rufus lives and it's a good
thing... he IS Rome's best guard.

                    RUFUS
Thank you sir. That is the greatest
compliment I have ever received and
it means so much that you would
honor me with those words from your
breath.

                    GREGG
          (whispering)
Dude, did you hear that thank you?
It was so sincere. I think there's
a tear going down his face.

                    MATTHIAS
          (whispering)
You're right. He has a single tear
going down his face like he's
Denzel Washington.

                    GREGG
          (whispering)
These people are crazy.

                    TITUS
Okay, now that the formalities are
out of the way, let's get down to
business.

                    MATTHIAS
          Hey tell you what, you and Mike
          talk while we take in this awesome
          city.

                    MIKE
          Wait, what?

                    GREGG
          Yeah, we're like his less important
          somethings. So we shouldn't be
          here.

                    MIKE
          Why are you doing this? There is
          absolutely no reason why you would
          want to split up.

                    MATTHIAS
          Well its happening. There was a bar
          we passed on the way in, we can
          meet up in an hour... Bye...

                    TITUS
          What strange companions you have.

                    MIKE
          Yeah they're assholes.

                                        FOOTSTEPS AWAY

EXT. STREETS OF ROME - DAY

                                        GLITCH SFX

                    ORATOR
          So they split up. Nearly 100% of
          the population wouldn't have made
          that decision under those
          circumstances but they did and no
          one could ever grow to understand
          how they made their decisions. Not
          even them.

                                        GLITCH SFX

          As Gregg and Matthias walked out of
          the room to an uncertain world Mike
          stood there, very angry, because
          they left him all alone with the
          Emperor of Rome. To him this was no
          different than being left at a
          birthday party for a child you're
          not even related to.

GLITCH SFX

EXT. STREETS OF ROOM - DAY

CROWDED STREETS OF ROME

                    GREGG
          Hey, why did we ditch Mike?

                    MATTHIAS
          I don't know, that old guy started
          talking and my brain was like "No
          get out dude get out".

                    GREGG
          I think I felt that too because I
          did like a Forrest Gump where I
          just followed your lead... I feel
          bad for Mike.

                    MATTHIAS
          I don't... We have been doing
          everything he wants to do all day.

                    GREGG
          Not really.

                    MATTHIAS
          I know but hey, we're out and
          about, there's got to be something
          fun to do for no money in a land we
          know nothing about... Wow, we
          really didn't think this through.

                    RUFUS
          I could help find anything you
          need.

                    GREGG & MATTHIAS
          Whoa!

                    GREGG
          Where the hell did you come from?!

                    MATTHIAS
          Yeah don't sneak up on people. Not
          cool brah.

                    RUFUS
          I was walking beside you this whole
          time.

                    MATTHIAS
Well put a bell on or something.

                    GREGG
Hey now that you're here, what can
you do to get us laid?

                    RUFUS
Are you in need of rest?

                    MATTHIAS
No, we want to do some bangin'

                    RUFUS
You want to fight someone?

                    GREGG
No, chick's dude.

                    RUFUS
You want to watch some cock fights?

                    MATTHIAS
No, get some ass to plow.

                    RUFUS
We do have donkeys and our fields
could use tending but you're noble
men, you shouldn't do such work.

                    GREGG
We're talking about Sex.

                    RUFUS
This way.

                    MATTHIAS
With girls.

                    RUFUS
Oh. Then this way.

                                        GLITCH SFX

                    ORATOR
Rufus took Gregg and Matthias to
the brand new Titus bath house. It
was said to have the finest women
and food. Gregg and Matthias were
especially excited when Rufus told
them it was all covered by the
Emperor.

                                        GLITCH SFX

INT. TITUS BATHHOUSES - DAY

                CULUS
Hello Rufus and my new friends.
Welcome to the Titus bathhouse. I
am Culus, I handle the day to day
operations.

                GREGG
Okay, everyone is butt ass naked in
here.

                RUFUS
Hello Culus. These are guests of
the Emperor, Gregg and Matthias.
Treat them well.

                CULUS
Of course and would you be having
your usual today?

                RUFUS
Better make it ten girls today.

                MATTHIAS
You're going to do 10 girls?

                RUFUS
Yeah. I'm a bit under the weather
so ten is all I can handle right
now... Anyway, I'll be back. You
boys enjoy yourselves.

                GREGG
Wow.... This guy's sick and doesn't
even care if he gives it to anyone.

                MATTHIAS
I dislike him more and more as the
day goes on.

                CULUS
Gentlemen how can I help you have
the best time of you lives?

                GREGG
You know what? I was about the
bangin' until I saw everyone naked
and now I'm thinking food.

                CULUS
Very well sir. I will escort you
momentarily to the dining hall.

                        GREGG
Thanks, see you in a few Tee.

                        CULUS
And you sir?

                        MATTHIAS
Oh I still want to bang.

                        CULUS
Bang what?

                        MATTHIAS

Sex.

                        CULUS
Yes this way sir.

                        MATTHIAS
With girls.

                        CULUS
Oh, this way then sir.

                        MATTHIAS
Where were you going to take me if
I didn't say girls? You know what
never mind.

                        CULUS
And here we are. Pick any you want.

                        MATTHIAS
Cool... I like how all their
boobies are out... it's a nice
touch.

                        CULUS
Ladies don't be rude, introduce
yourselves.

                        MATTHIAS
No don't do that. I'm picking you.

                        CULUS
Oh I see, you're a skinny chaser.
Not many people like that sort of
thing.

                        MATTHIAS
Oh ya, I'm weird... Give me a room
and take a hike.

                    ORATOR
So Matthias and his newly acquired
prostitute went up to their room.
Matthias never had a prostitute
before but he said to himself when
in Rome

in fact he said that to himself 6
times that day and laughed at
everyone of them.

          GLITCH SFX DOOR GLITCH SFX

                                        KISSING SFX

                    MATTHIAS
Wow your breath is bad.

                 THE PROSTITUTE
Yeah... and your breath is not.

                    MATTHIAS
It's called a mint, invent it
please.

                 THE PROSTITUTE
Lets get to it then.

                    MATTHIAS
Okay lets get that skirt or
whatever the hell this is called
off... and oh my good that's a lot
of pubic hair.

                 THE PROSTITUTE
What seems to be the problem?

                    MATTHIAS
What's the problem?... Um, I don't
know, maybe the Chewbacca diaper
you got on.

                 THE PROSTITUTE
Do you not like it?

                    MATTHIAS
Come on, it goes up to your belly
button... You know what... I can
work with this.

                 THE PROSTITUTE
Well then come and ravish me.

                    MATTHIAS
Oh ya baby, spread those legs
and... what the fuck is that
smell!?

                    THE PROSTITUTE
What is it now?

                    MATTHIAS
Oh I don't know, maybe it's the
fact your vagina smells like it
died 2 weeks ago from old age.

                    THE PROSTITUTE
How is it supposed to smell?

                    MATTHIAS
Like fish, not a haunted
aquarium... This sucks... I should
have went with Gregg.

                    ORATOR
Matthias was wrong when he made
that statement. Gregg was not
having a good time either.

                    GLITCH SFX
                                        SOUNDS OF PUKING.

                    CULUS
The dinning hall and Vomitorium
sir.

                    GREGG
ya know what I'm good on food...No
thank you.

INT. ROMAN BAR - DAY

                    BAR AMBIENCE
                                        GLITCH SFX

                    ORATOR
later they all met up at a local
bar in the center of the city. Mike
was the last to show up. Unlike
them he had a rather pleasant time
with the Emperor. He would never
admit this to anyone.

                                        GLITCH SFX

                    MIKE
Wh wh wh what up.

                    GREGG
Dude what are you smoking?

                    MIKE
Opium... Want some? The Emperor had
tons of it... He's fucking crazy.

                    MATTHIAS
Yes.

                    GREGG
Do you have money? We ditched Rufus
so we have no way to buy stuff.

                    MIKE
I got you... Titus gave me some
walking around money.

                    MATTHIAS
Nice... Lets drink until I can fuck
a Roman woman. Even though I might
die of alcohol poisoning first.

                    MIKE
OK but lets be careful alcohol is
stronger in this time.

                    GREGG
I think ill be fine.

                    MIKE
Cool, lets do it.

                                        GLITCH SFX

                    ORATOR
So the boys drank until blackout
occurred which was not unusual for
them. What was unusual was them
waking up in a jail cell...let me
clarify that... it was unlike them
to wake up in a jail cell in 80 AD.

                                        GLITCH SFX

INT. ROMAN JAIL - DAY

ROMAN JAIL AMBIENCE

                GREGG
Dude what? Bars, that's not good.

                MATTHIAS
Are we in jail?

                MIKE
Ya dude... I warned you about the
alcohol

                              FOOTSTEPS APPROACHING

                RUFUS
I see you're awake.

                MIKE
Hey Rufus, good to see ya. Can you
get us out of here.

                RUFUS
Do you know what you three did last
night? Matthias, you were walking
up to women saying "Can you toss
this Caesar salad"... then you
would proceed to pull your butt
apart... and Mike you on three
occasions would throw a sword at
the wall and scream ... "are you
not entertained?"... Gregg, you
showed your penis to the whole bar
which is not a crime but being
circumcised means you're a Jew so
we locked you up with them.

                MATTHIAS
So.. Big deal we're diplomats. You
can't just imprison us.

                RUFUS
Yes I can and you three will be
fighting in tomorrow's games at the
Colosseum... I look forward to
seeing you compete...

                MIKE
What a dick.

                    MATTHIAS
          Great. I'm going to be killed by a
          gladiator and it's not even an
          American gladiator. This is your
          fault Mike.

                    MIKE
          My fault? What about you? "I'm
          Matthias I can do whatever I want
          like a Nazi."

                    GREGG
          Hey we should kill Hitler after
          this.

                    MIKE AND MATTHIAS
          Shut up Gregg. You shut up too.

                    GREGG
          Jinx on you both.

                    MIKE
          It doesn't work like that.

                    GREGG
          Yes it does.

                                                  GLITCH SFX

                    ORATOR
          by this time they were having one
          of their legendary arguments... I
          will fast forward because the
          subject matter will change so much
          that very few people on earth could
          follow.

                                                  GLITCH SFX

          This happened a lot even when they
          were kids. I suppose that's why
          they became such good friends. They
          were exceptionally good at driving
          people away except each other...

                                                  GLITCH SFX

          INT. ROMAN JAIL - LATER THAT NIGHT

                    MIKE
          I'm not aruging with you about what
          the best breakfast cereal is
          anymore

                    GREGG
He's right this is childish

                    MATTHIAS
Wait... when did it get dark?

                    MIKE
Holy shit dude it is dark. We've
been arguing for like 9 hours.

                    GREGG
The guard is gone.

                    MIKE
Sweet... I can pick this old lock
no problem.

                                        LOCK PICKING SFX

                    RUFUS
What are you doing.

                    MIKE
Whoa, dude!

                    MATTHIAS
There you go again, sneaking up on
people. I mean, what's your
problem.

                    RUFUS
What were you just doing?

                    GREGG
Relax you broken record, we're not
trying to escape or anything.

                    RUFUS
Its okay, I'm here to help you
escape.

                    MIKE
What?

                    GREGG
No way.

                    MATTHIAS
Really?

                    MIKE
Why would you do that?

                    RUFUS
Because I like you guys... you
treat me like a person and not a
servant like everyone else... You
know, just last week I was with--

                    MATTHIAS
Cool just open the door.

                    RUFUS
Right.

                                    KEY IN LOCK SFX

                    MIKE
OK lead the way dude, I don't know
where the fuck I'm going.

                    RUFUS
Come on this way

                    MIKE
Wait... I feel like if I don't say
this all of us will die. We want to
escape from this prison And LEAVE
ROME...

                    RUFUS
Oh then let's go this way.

                                    WALKING DOWN HALL

                    RUFUS
        (beat)
It's Not much further.

                    ROMAN GUARDS
You four stop right there!

                    MIKE
Oh man, guards.

                    RUFUS
Let me talk to them.

                    ROMAN GUARDS
Oh hello Rufus. How are you my
friend?

                    RUFUS
I'm well and you.

                    ROMAN GUARDS
Still alive thank the gods... What
are you doing down here?

                    RUFUS
Well, I was just...

                    MATTHIAS
Breaking us out of jail. Run!

                              RUNNING FOOTSTEPS X3

                    MIKE
You just pushed Rufus in to the
guards!

                    MATTHIAS
Yup!

                    MIKE
Good move

                    GREGG
Lets haul ass back to the
time-crapper I'm done with this
place.

                              GLITCH SFX

                    ORATOR
they escaped the jail and the
streets of Rome and ran straight to
the time machine... With about 300
Roman soldiers right behind them.
the soldiers giving chase were very
impressed on how fast they could
run. So they began to shoot arrows
at them.

                              ARROW SFX

at this point Mike realized this
was the second time he had traveled
into the past and the second time
he had to run for his life. This
revelation upset him a great deal.

                    GLITCH SFX

                              ANGRY MOB SFX

                    MIKE
Shit, there shooting arrows.

                              SHOOTING ARROW SFX

                    GREGG
We're almost there.

                    MATTHIAS
Quick! Open the door.

                    DOOR OPEN

                                                ARROW SFX

                    MIKE
Close the fucking door!

                    MATTHIAS
Sorry didn't know that was my job.

                    GREGG
You were the last one in.

                    MIKE
Oh my god stop talking

                    GREGG
Okay get us out of here.

                    MIKE
Oh no no no no no!

                    MATTHIAS
What's wrong?

                    MIKE
An arrow hit the control panel. I
can't punch in a time or place. If
I turn the machine on we could end
up anywhere in time.

                    GREGG
We can't stay here. Right before we
ran in here I flicked them off.

                    MIKE
This isn't happening.

                    MATTHIAS
Don't you have a return to home
button on this thing.

                    GREGG
Just go dude I can hear them out
there.

                    MIKE
Okay. There's no place like home,
there's no place like home, there's
no place like home.

                    GREGG
Come on just do it.

                    MIKE
I already did.

                                        FAN MOTOR DYING

                    MATTHIAS
Dude, this time machine making no
noise is starting to piss me off.
I'd like to know when I'm being
hurled through time and space.

                    GREGG
You think we made it home?

                    MIKE
There's only one way to find out.

                                        DOOR OPEN SFX

                    MIKE
I'm going to say no...

                                        WAR SFX

                    RUFUS
What just happened?

            MIKE & GREGG & MATTHAIS
WHOAH!!

                    MIKE
What the hell is your problem!...
and how did you get in here? Last
time I checked you were being
manhandled by four guards.

                    RUFUS
I managed to kill all of the
guards. I was not more than 20 feet
away from you the whole time, I was
even shouting your names.

                    GREGG
That's cool man glad to see you're
alive, but have you noticed that
flag hanging on the wall dude?

                    RUFUS
My word That is a beautiful flag
which Empire does it represent?

                                        AIRCRAFT DIVING SFX

               MIKE
Nazis.

                                        GLITCH SFX

               ORATOR
and that was how Mike and his
fellow teleporters accidentally
took a roman soldier to the 2nd
World War... But that's a whole
different set of files all
together...

                                        GLITCH SFX

I hope this information has helped
your research... please feel free
to check my data banks from time to
time... As you further your
research, you will come to learn
more and more about the worlds
first team of Teleporterz.

               FOOTSTEPS AWAY
               POWER DOWN SFX

                                   FADE OUT

ENDING CREDITS

                         END CREDITS MUSIC

          THE VOICE OF THE CLEVELAND RADIO PLAYERS
You have been listening to The
Cleveland Radio Players Performance
of Teleporterz... A Sci-Fi series
by Michael Lawrence... Directed by
Milton Horowitz ... Starring...

               DEANNA DIONNE

               LOGAN SMITH
               CORY SHY
               ANDREW JURCAK

               JACK HUNT

               DAVID FLYNT
               CHARLES HARGRAVE
               KATIE SEAVEY (KTCV)

                        KAT BI
GIOVANNI CASTIGLIONE
                ... and my name is Denny
                Castiglione Ladies and Gentlemen...
                Teleporterz was recorded at Bad
                Racket Studio... made in part by
                Gotta Groove Records... To purchase
                Teleporterz as an audiobook, MP3 or
                twelve inch vinyl record please
                visit
                www.ClevelandRadioPlayers.com...
                copyright 2015

Rights and Royalties

Originally adapted for the radio and performed
by The Cleveland Radio Players

Directed by Milton Matthew Horowitz

Recorded at Bad Racket Studios

For more information on performance rights and
royalties, or to listen to Teleporterz:
Rome80AD as a radio play, please visit
www.ClevelandRadioPlayers.com

www.ingramcontent.com/pod-product-compliance
Lightning Source LLC
Chambersburg PA
CBHW080812120626
46556CB00009B/3296